Rocket Says
SPEAK UP!

Written by
Nathan Bryon

Illustrated by
Dapo Adeola

RANDOM HOUSE 🏠 NEW YORK

To Noah, Oscar, Finley, Athena, Orla—I can't wait to watch you all grow up and speak up! (RIP BIG C—a real one, woof woof.) —N.B.

To Joe, Monica, Chloe, Sallyanne, and Nathan. Thanks for being the absolute BEST team to work with. And to all our readers for showing us love. #TeamRocketForLife —D.A.

Text copyright © 2023 by Nathan Bryon
Jacket art and interior illustrations copyright © 2023 by Dapo Adeola

All rights reserved. Published in the United States by Random House Children's Books, a division of Penguin Random House LLC, New York. Originally published in paperback in a slightly different form by Puffin Books, an imprint of Penguin Random House Children's Books UK, a division of Penguin Random House UK, London, in 2023.

Random House and the colophon are registered trademarks of Penguin Random House LLC.

Visit us on the Web! rhcbooks.com

Educators and librarians, for a variety of teaching tools, visit us at RHTeachersLibrarians.com

Library of Congress Cataloging-in-Publication Data is available upon request.
ISBN 978-0-593-43126-9 (trade) — ISBN 978-0-593-43127-6 (ebook)

MANUFACTURED IN CHINA
10 9 8 7 6 5 4 3 2 1
First American Edition

Tomorrow is my favorite day of the week.
IT'S NEW BOOK DAY!

Every Friday after school, Mom, Jamal (he's my big brother), and I go to the library to borrow our new books for the week.

DID YOU KNOW . . . there are over two million new books published every year?

I read more books than anyone else in my family. I used to find reading difficult, but the more I do it, the better I get.

Jamal says I eat books for breakfast, lunch, and dinner, but the thought of eating books is gross!

Eurgh

Jamal says he likes books about history,
but we only ever see him reading
books about romance.

I **LOVE** all kinds of books . . .

books that teach me unbelievable facts,

books that take me on adventures,

and books about great people who changed the world.

I've just been reading all about Rosa Parks.

DID YOU KNOW . . .
Rosa Parks led a famous protest? She had been told to give up her seat on the bus to a white man—just because of the color of her skin—and she said **NO!**

The library is in a **HUGE** building that used to
be a theater. It's a bit old and dusty, but I love it.

There are books
EVERYWHERE!

The library is mainly for quiet reading,
but sometimes authors and illustrators come to
read stories—and then it can get quite **NOISY!**

Today, Layla the librarian hands me a book she thinks I'll love. She always has the best recommendations.

She also gives me a party invitation!

I LOVE PARTIES!

But Layla says it's a **GOODBYE** party. There isn't enough money to keep the library open, so it has to close down.

OH NO!

The next day, everybody goes to the library-closing party. But it doesn't feel like a party.

There is food—
but no one's eating.

There are books—but no one's reading.

Everyone just looks . . . sad.
Nobody wants the library
to close.

There must be
something we can do!

On Monday at school, I start **SPEAKING UP** about libraries and how wonderful they are.

DID YOU KNOW . . . one overdue library book was returned after 288 years?

DID YOU KNOW . . . there are libraries in Portugal with families of bats that eat book-damaging bugs?

By the end of the day everyone in my class wants to stop the library from closing too.

But what do we do? What can we do?
We need to **SPEAK UP!** But how?

I've got it!

We'll have a peaceful protest—like Rosa Parks did!

We work together to get prepared and spread the word.
Our teachers, our parents, and Layla the librarian all help.

And by the weekend, we're ready to go!

"SAVE OUR LIBRARY!"

Lots of people join our peaceful protest outside the library.

They're all wearing my favorite outfit—we **look** amazing.
We're so loud we can probably be heard from the moon!
With everyone **SPEAKING UP** together, surely someone will listen.

After the peaceful protest
there is good news and bad news.

The good news is that everyone is talking about our protest—
it's even on TV and the internet.

The bad news is that day after day after day . . .
nothing has changed. The library is still closing.

NEWS

Library closing down

Breaking news . . . Break

What was the point?

HEADL

But one day the mail comes.
No one ever sends me letters!

And it's not just one or two—there are hundreds.

They're from people who saw the peaceful protest,
and they're amazing. . . .

Dear Rocket,
I saw your protest from my bedroom window
the other day, and I was super inspired by
how you got everyone in the community to
care about the library. That library is one
of my favorite places in the whole world,
and I want to help you save it!

Noah

While I'm reading the letters, the doorbell rings. . . .

And it's the mayor of our town!

She explains that people around the world were
inspired by our protest, and lots of them have
given money to help save the library.

She thanks me for **SPEAKING UP** and
gives me an invitation to a celebration.

This sounds like a party I definitely want to go to!

The library celebration is **AWESOME!**
The mayor tells us that enough money was raised
to refurbish the library and buy lots of new books.

There's food—and **everyone's eating!**

There are books—and **everyone's** reading!

Suddenly we hear a loud **beeeeeeeep!** What's that?

It's Layla the librarian with a **HUGE** bus!

The money people raised also helped to buy a new traveling library that lives **IN** the bus. Layla says we can all help out— bringing books to people everywhere.

"I'm so proud of you, Rocket," says Mom.
"Never stop **SPEAKING UP!**"

I'm proud of me too—and of everyone.
I'm so glad we all spoke up together.

DID YOU KNOW . . .
one day you're going to
write a book that changes the
world? And people will read
it in the library!

Here's how **YOU** can **SPEAK UP**
and make a difference!

READ UP

Find books that inspire you! Here are some suggestions:

Stand Up! Speak Up! by Andrew Joyner

Enough! 20 Protesters Who Changed America by Emily Easton,
illustrated by Ziyue Chen

Vote for Our Future! by Margaret McNamara,
illustrated by Micah Player

SPEAK UP

Here are three tips to empower you to use your voice:

Stand up for what you believe in—find a cause that matters to you!

Team up with others—a chorus of voices is more likely to be heard!

Never give up! Change can take time, so don't be discouraged
if you don't see results right away.

TAKE ACTION

For more information on how **YOU** can get involved in your community,
visit rootsandshoots.org/for-youth.